TALES from The CELTIC COUNTRIES

First impression: 1999
Fourth impression: 2005
© Copyright Rhiannon Ifans and Y Lolfa Cyf., 1999

Illustrations: Margaret Jones
Graphic Designer: Olwen Fowler

ISBN: 0 86243 501 3

Printed, published and bound in Wales by
Y Lolfa Cyf., Talybont, Ceredigion SY24 5AP;
e-mail ylolfa@ylolfa.co.uk
website http://www.ylolfa.com
phone (01970) 832 304
fax 832 782
isdn 832 813

Published with the support of the Arts Council of Wales

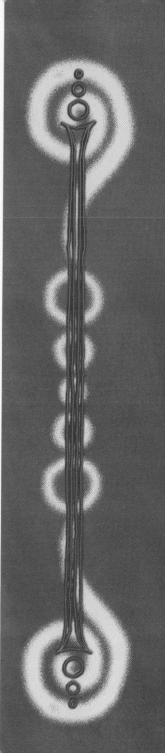

TALES from THE CELTIC COUNTRIES

Rhiannon Ifans

y Lolfa

To

Gwyddno, Seiriol and Einion

Acknowledgements

I wish to acknowledge assistance of various kinds afforded during the preparation of this volume by the late Emeritus Professor J.E. Caerwyn Williams, Emeritus Professor R.M. Jones, Mrs Rita Williams, and Dafydd Ifans. Thanks are due also to Robat Gruffudd at whose suggestion I wrote this book, and to the General Editor of Y Lolfa, Lefi Gruffudd, for his assistance and forbearance.

Contents

WALES

GWYDDNO'S SONG

If ever you visit Cardigan Bay on a dark, squally evening you will find the sea restless and disturbed, and brown seaweed like crab's claws riding the waves. But on a calm evening you will find the sea peaceful, crabs sitting leisurely on its shore, and large sheets of seaweed glinting lazily in the sun. In that quiet close of day, if you stand very, very still, you might hear church bells ringing beneath the waves. For, centuries ago, there was a land called Maes Gwyddno where Cardigan Bay lies today, a land which, much later on, became known as Cantre'r Gwaelod.

The king of that land was Gwyddno Garan Hir, Gwyddno Longshank, and in his castle was a huge party room. In that room were a thousand and one drinking-horns, goblets, and plates of heavy gold. And in that enormous room they often held frenzied parties - singing and dancing, eating and

drinking, until the early hours of the morning. That is just how it was one dark winter's night. The coastline was sad and empty, with no need for map or chart as all the citizens of Maes Gwyddno were at home huddled by the fire, or preparing for the party to be held in Gwyddno's castle.

Everyone, that is, apart from the watchmen. The kingdom of Maes Gwyddno was lower than sea level and a high embankment had been built to prevent the sea from submerging the state. Gwyddno had appointed watchmen to care for the embankment. Their chief concern was to walk the length of the wall checking its safety. If the sea ate into the stone wall it was the watchmen's responsibility to repair the damage. And if there was any danger at all of the sea ripping through the holes and cavities in the embankment and drowning the land, they were to ring the tower bell for help. Then, the people of Maes Gwyddno had to race to the wall to assist with the rebuilding of the embankment. They would plug the holes with pebbles and boulders so that the kingdom of Maes Gwyddno was safe once again. But that didn't happen very often.

On this dark night the keeper of the dike was exceptionally busy. His name was Seithenyn and he had noticed the wind rising as the sun was setting. By the time the party was to begin, a gusty wind was ploughing the sea. Currents pummelled against the embankment. Spray was tossed over the high wall, freezing the very muscles of Seithenyn's face. But he carried on with his work in a cheerful mood, watching and waiting, waiting and watching. He held a flaming torch in his hand to get a better view of things. No, there was no danger at all. Everything was exactly as it should be.

But out in the eye of the storm Seithenyn was almost numb with cold. Warm mead! That was the answer. He would run into the castle kitchens for a drop of mead. He struggled up the path to the castle, but the wind was so strong Seithenyn could hardly move. He had to dig his sword into the ground and catch hold of it several times. Otherwise, he would have been swept clean away.

Having hauled himself up the path inch by inch through the raging storm, Seithenyn reached the heavy kitchen doors. The bolts were slid open. Once inside the kitchen the warm mead slipped luxuriously down Seithenyn's throat. After the third tumblerful he had clean forgotten the dike, the sea, and the storm. He had nothing but mead and peat fires on his mind.

But however great a fuss was made of the party, there was yet more fuss in store. When the wind was at its most treacherous, and the sea at its most ferocious, Seithenyn would have seen in the light of his flaming torch, had he been down at the great wall, a faint dribble of salt water trickling between two stones. A drip at a time, then two drops at a time, until the drips became a flood; the sea was submerging Maes Gwyddno slowly but relentlessly. The wind ripped the bell from its tower and the tongue rang out into the darkness, but to no avail. No one heard it from the comfort of the castle, behind the heavy doors. Harps had hummed them all asleep, and

the mead had their heads in a whirl. Seithenyn, the drunken reveller, was even sillier than the rest.

And that is how the wind drove the sea through the holes in the dike. That is how the waves rushed up the path to the castle's heavy doors. That is how the sea-water whipped through the castle windows and under its doors, drowning every man and dog in the kingdom. All except one.

When King Gwyddno Garan Hir saw the sea submerging his land and realised he could do nothing but save his own skin, he ran as fast as his legs would carry him, up into the mountains. There, his sad, sad song could be heard alternating with a long, long sigh. And if ever you stand close to where Gwyddno stood that night you may hear him, even today, whispering his song at sunset. But you would have to be very lucky indeed to hear the church bells ringing beneath the waves.

The Lady of the Woods

Einion ap Gwalchmai was married to Angharad, the daughter of Ednyfed Fychan, and they lived happily together in the holding of Trefeilyr on the Isle of Anglesey. But one fine morning, as Einion walked through Trefeilyr woods, he met another very beautiful woman and fell head over heels in love with her.

'Good day,' said Einion, anxious to please. She smiled a winning smile and within five seconds they were lovers. It was then that Einion noticed – she had hooves instead of feet.

'Well I never!' he exclaimed with displeasure. Then he lost his temper, but it was no use. The girl had cast a spell over him. He would have to follow in her every step, every day of his life. Einion pleaded with her to allow him to return home to say goodbye to his wife and son.

'Of course!' said the Lady of the Woods, 'but I must come too. I'll make myself invisible. Only you will be able to see me.'

And so it was that Einion and the Lady of the Woods went in search of Angharad and her son, Einion. Angharad was at home, looking the exact replica of a slovenly old witch, her hair bedraggled, her fingernails black as soot. Einion yearned for the old times when he had loved Angharad until his heart ached. But the spell was too strong for Einion and he gave up fighting it.

'I must leave home now, Angharad. I must leave you too, Einion my dear,' he said. All three wept bitter tears but under the eagle eye of the Lady of the Woods, Einion could change nothing. He owned a gold ring, which he broke in two halves. One half he put in his pocket, the other he gave Angharad.

'Goodbye!' said Einion sadly. 'I hope these two halves become one before too long!'

He followed the Lady of the Woods over hills and mountains, rivers and streams, without knowing where he was headed and without taking the least bit of interest in anything but the half band of gold in his pocket. One morning at break of day he looked at the ring and thought once again of Angharad, the apple of his eye. In order to feel closer to Angharad he placed the half band on the pupil of his own eye and pulled an eyelid over the ring. As quick as lightning a white horse galloped towards him and a man wearing white robes rode on its back.

'What are you doing?' asked the man in white robes as soon as he saw the ring in Einion's eye.

'Missing Angharad, my wife, and Einion, my little son.'

'Would you like to see them?'

'More than anything in the world.'

'Hop up behind me and we'll ride over to Trefeilyr.' The Lady of the Woods was nowhere to be seen, only her hoof-tracks heading north.

'Why are you so sad?' asked the rider. Einion told him his unhappy story.

'Hold on to this white stick and make a wish,' said the man in white robes. 'What do you yearn for more than anything?'

'I miss Angharad very much but I miss seeing the Lady of the Woods even more,' said Einion, still under the spell of that temptress.

In the blinking of an eyelid he saw an ugly witch standing before him. Saliva drivelled from between her black teeth, a loose cough roared in her throat, and what with that and the gnashing of her thin bones, it wasn't a pretty sight. Indeed, she was a thousand times uglier than the ugliest thing in the world. Einion was so terrified of her he was almost sick. The man in white robes threw his cloak over Einion's head and so the spell was broken.

When Einion came to himself once more he was back home in Trefeilyr, safe in his own house. But no one there knew him at all, and Einion knew no one in Trefeilyr.

This is what had really happened. The witch had travelled north with all speed – to Trefeilyr on the Isle of Anglesey, to speak to Angharad. Pretending to be a rich and important young man, the Lady of the Woods had coaxed Angharad to marry her. She had given Angharad a letter telling her that Einion had died in Scandinavia nine years earlier. Angharad had grieved long over Einion's disappearance, but was gradually growing accustomed to the fact that he would never return. She fell under the spell of the charming young man and agreed to marry him.

Angharad bought an expensive wedding dress and all the trappings. Expensive food was ordered for the banquet. She invited the cream of the land to the church and ordered the best musicians to play at the wedding feast. When the young man saw Angharad's harp he tried to play music, but not one person in Trefeilyr could tune the harp for him.

When the wedding party was about to set off for the church, Einion arrived home. Angharad didn't recognise him. All she could see was a feeble old man in ragged clothes, trembling with age.

'Will you roast this meat while we're up at the church, old man?'

asked Angharad.

'I will,' said Einion holding on firmly to his white stick.

When the wedding party returned from church, the harp still untuned, Einion tried his hand at it and succeeded in no time at all. He played one of Angharad's favourite melodies. Angharad was very surprised and asked him his name.

'Einion ap Gwalchmai,' said the old man, and sang a few verses. But Angharad was still firmly under the spell of the rich and important young man, her new husband. She could remember nothing. Einion placed the white stick in Angharad's hand and instantly Angharad could see her new husband as the huge drivelling monster that he really was. She fainted in fright.

Einion nursed her tenderly. And when, at long last, Angharad opened her eyes, there was no one in Trefeilyr Hall except herself, Einion, and their little son. The house and harp and all their other possessions were exactly as they had been in the old days. The spell had vanished. Even the gold ring was in one piece on her finger again.

IRELAND

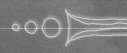

VALLEY OF THE WOLVES

Strange things happened in the Ireland of long ago. People disappeared without trace, birds sang through the long nights, and when everything was calm and peaceful, monsters rose out of the lakes - sometimes. Very odd. Ireland wasn't at all a safe place in olden times.

One day it happened that Caílte and Cas Corach were chatting about some of the unfortunate things that had happened to them.

'Oh dear, I'm head over heels in trouble once more,' said Cas Corach.

'Isn't Ireland a terrible place to be these days?' said Caílte, shaking his head.

'You wouldn't believe it, but someone is persecuting me,' said Cas Corach in a thin small voice. 'They're picking on me, so they are, and I'll let you in on the tale.' He leaned forward for effect, but his hands lay limp over the side of his chair.

'Of course you know the whereabouts of the Cave of Cruacha. Well, every year of late, wolves have run out of that cave intent on killing my sheep. Three she-wolves! Before I know where I am they've killed my sheep and are back in the safety of the cave. Oh! I wish I could get even with those fiends!'

'What do you know about them? Would you recognize them if you saw them again?' asked Caílte.

'What do I know about them! They're the daughters of Airitech, and he was the last of the Company of Grief. His daughters are the spitting image of him - grief is all I ever gained at their hands,' grumbled Cas Corach. By now his fingers were working the arm of his chair such was his hatred for the wolves which ravaged his flock.

'As soon as these daughters are turned into wolves they wreak havoc on the countryside.' Cas Corach was beside himself. 'They have no compassion for man or beast. Well, apart from one society of people.'

'And what would that be?' questioned Caílte.

'If they see either a harpist or a lute-player all is well, but they won't go near anyone else.'

'Where do the she-wolves go by day?'

'To the top of Carn Bricre,' answered Cas Corach.

'Then why don't you go up there tomorrow to play your harp?' suggested Caílte.

Cas Corach did just that. First thing in the morning Cas Corach jumped out of bed and was up Carn Bricre in a flash. He played his harp from dawn till dusk. The three she-wolves ventured nearer and nearer; they lay down before him and were entranced by the music of his harp. Before Cas Corach could attack, the three she-wolves disappeared with the light of day.

Cas Corach was very disappointed.

He told his bitter tale to Caílte. 'Go back there tomorrow,' urged Caílte. 'Take some soldiers with you, and hide them all over the mountain. When the she-wolves appear tell them your music is more rhythmic to human ears than it is to wolves'. That should persuade them to change their shape. Girls are easier to kill than wild wolves.'

At the crack of dawn Cas Corach climbed Carn Bricre and positioned his men behind clumps of gorse and in the shadow of great rocks the length and breadth of Carn Bricre. Caílte himself was amongst the band of followers. Caílte hid himself in the mossy ruins of a tumbledown cottage. Would the she-wolves return?

Indeed they did – all three! They lay down at leisure, to the accompaniment of sweet music. One she-wolf lay down her head on her front paws. Cas Corach ventured a greeting.

'If you are truly the young girls you say you are, you would enjoy these songs far more in your human form,' cajoled Cas Corach.

The she-wolves were dubious. They considered the suggestion for a great length of time. By degrees they took off their black hairy skins and were even more delighted with the sad, plaintive songs. As soon as they were lying side by side, paws in line, lazing to the sway of the music, Caílte arose quietly from his hide-out. He set a shining, sharp-edged spear in his catapult and aimed at his prey. The spearhead moved through the air at great speed, piercing first one girl, then the second, before boring through the third so that all three were wincing and writhing like pieces of meat cooking on a skewer.

Cas Corach cut off their heads one by one. The heads rolled down the side of the valley, never to bother Cas Corach or his sheep ever again. And that is how the Valley of the Wolves was named, the valley on the north side of Carn Bricre, in Ireland.

HOW CÚCHULAINN GOT HIS NAME

Long ago there lived in Ireland a jolly little pedlar who was always hard at work travelling here and there selling his wares. He was sure to have something to tickle the fancy of even his grumpiest customer - yellow ribbons, crimson ribbons; silk shirts, cotton shirts; pegs and pat-balls; draughts and dominos; buttons and beads; riddles and reels - EVERYTHING you could possibly wish for.

He decided to spend the day at the races. He would set up his stall in the enclosure. Since the whole of Ireland loved horse-racing he would sell his entire stock in double-quick time and be a very rich man.

The horses galloped like the wind, some black, some white, others tearing past him in a flash of reddish-brown.

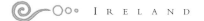

'Did you ever see anything move faster than these horses?' asked a stranger to the pedlar. The pedlar ignored him.

'Did you ever see anything move faster than these horses?' asked the stranger for the second time. The pedlar still ignored him.

'If you don't answer my question in two shakes of a rat's tail, I'll cut off your head,' said the man in exasperation.

'My wife can run faster than these horses,' said the pedlar. 'Your horses run at a snail's pace compared with my wife.'

'You impudent man! Bring your wife here tomorrow and we'll race her against my best horses. If she doesn't win by a mile, I'll cut off your head!'

The pedlar's wife wasn't amused. She wasn't feeling one hundred per cent, and wasn't in the mood for racing against horses. She told the pedlar she was ill and couldn't run ten steps.

'Then you might as well poison me this minute,' said the pedlar. 'I'll be dead and buried by tomorrow night in any case.'

The pedlar's wife relented. After giving him a good piece of her mind for being so rash she went to bed and slept until dawn. When she reached the racecourse, tension was high.

'Three races,' declared the judges. 'The best of three.'

The pedlar's wife stood at the starting-line alongside six mighty

horses jostling for position, each one keen to be the first to push its nostrils past the finishing-post. Who won? It was a hard and tiring race, but Hurrah! the pedlar's wife won. The pedlar's wife won the second also. Hurrah! Hurrah! She was the clear champion! The pedlar kept his head, and his wife kept the golden cup. But she had gained more than she had bargained for. Immediately following the race, a son was born to her. She wasn't very happy with that so she sold him to a gentleman standing close by.

'This is my lucky day – a gold cup and a fistful of coins!' rejoiced the pedlar's wife.

The child grew sturdy and strong and enjoyed sports of every kind: running, jumping, archery, and all the old games of Ireland. One day he beat his brothers at a ball game. They were infuriated.

'You have no right at all to beat us! You're only a pedlar's son, born at the races!'

The boy had known nothing of that and since his father was not at home to establish the truth the boy scurried away to find him. His father was visiting a friend. The friend kept a dog that would kill anyone who approached the farm without permission. When the boy rushed at the farm gate he put his hand on the gate-post to steady himself and jumped the fence. The dog attacked, fully intent on killing the trespasser, but the boy slapped the dog with the back of his hand and broke the dog's neck.

'Are you my father?' asked the boy.

'No. You're a pedlar's son,' replied the gentleman.

'But don't let your brothers mock you for it,' said his friend. 'You are a better son than they will ever be. But you have caused me great concern today, and a great loss. You have killed my dog - the best guard-dog in the world. You must remain here until the dog's puppies are old enough to guard my farm. Until that day dawns, the safety of the farm is your responsibility. Keep an eagle eye on this land, every nook and cranny.'

'What is your name?' the boy asked the dog-owner.

'Culann.'

'I'm sorry I caused you so much pain. I'll stay here with you, Culann, for a twelvemonth. I'll watch over this place diligently, and won't ask a penny in return.'

And that is how the boy came to be called Cúchulainn (Culann's dog) for his part in killing Culann's hound and guarding the farm in return.

BRITTANY

LITTLE FRIAR

AND LARGE FRIAR

Long ago in Bear in Brittany there lived two friars, Little Friar and Large Friar. Little Friar was a very small friar, who had very little riches. He owned just one small meadow which grazed just one small bullock. Large Friar was a very large friar, and had immense riches. He owned dozens of large meadows which grazed dozens of hefty beasts. Little Friar had a great mind but Large Friar's mind was minute.

One morning at breakfast, Large Friar told Little Friar that their meat was running low. 'There's nothing for it but to kill a bullock,' said Large Friar. But which one?

They decided to open each gate and kill whichever bullock escaped from the fields first. There was very little grass in Little Friar's meadow, and his bullock came rushing out ahead of the others in search of richer pastures.

It was killed and flayed, roasted and devoured in
no time at all.

'I'm off to Pontrew tomorrow to sell the hide,'
said Little Friar. He set off at midnight, far too early,
and of course he reached journey's end way before dawn.
He rested in the hedge-side, smoking. Soon he heard the
sound of men wrangling over the contents of a leather
bag. He peered through the hedge and there in the
cornfield were three massive men, each the size of an
elephant.

'Stop fighting over this booty,' said one cantankerous
man to the other, 'or the Devil will take you.'

That set Little Friar's mind ticking. He clothed
himself in the hide, set the horns straight, and jumped
on the men with an unearthly scream. The burglars
skedaddled off to the four corners of the earth and were
never seen again. Little Friar snatched the takings, every
single coin, and counted the proceeds there and then by
the light of the moon. One hundred *skoed!* A fortune!

It was high time Little Friar made his way to

Pontrew. There, he sold the hide for two *skoed*. He pushed his hands deep into his pockets. He was a happy man.

When Little Friar returned to the abbey to tell his tale, Large Friar was appalled. One hundred and two *skoed* for one hide! Incredible! Large Friar killed all his beasts, loaded the hides into the back of a cart, and pushed them every step of the way to Pontrew. Tanners from as far afield as Gwengamp flocked to see them.

'How much each?' called the tanners.

'One hundred *skoed*, plus two for the servant,' said Large Friar.

'Poppycock!' laughed the tanners, and walked away.

Large Friar realised his mistake. He went straight back to the abbey speaking indignantly of Little Friar's trickery.

'Rotten hand!' said the little rascal, 'but at least we have plenty of meat!'

A short time later, Little Friar's mother died. She was a native of Pontrew, and so Little Friar saddled his horse and carried her to Pontrew for burial. His mother weighed a ton, his horse was blind, and the road was never-ending. Little Friar rested in the hedge-side, smoking. Nearby were some yellow pears growing in a ripe garden.

That set Little Friar's mind ticking. He stood his mother under the pear tree clutching a golden pear in her hand. Little Friar jumped into the

garden with an unearthly scream: 'Thief! Thief!'

A man rushed out of the house and shot the old woman straight between the eyes.

'Murder! Murder!' cried Little Friar. 'You've murdered my mother!'

'Quiet will you!' called the man urgently. 'Name your price. I'll give you gold, but not a word to a soul about your mother. Don't bring in the law!'

'Seven hundred *skoed*,' said Little Friar.

'Done!'

Little Friar continued on his journey to Pontrew. Gradually he loosened his hold on the horse's reins, and the blind horse trampled all that lay in its path. The crowd shouted abuse at the old woman, urging her to keep better control over her horse, but the old woman never listened to a word they said. Soon, one scoundrel lost his temper and went at her hammer and tongs. The old woman fell to the floor.

'Murder! Murder!' cried Little Friar. 'You've murdered my mother!'

'Quiet will you!' called the man urgently. 'Name your price. I'll give you gold, but don't bring in the law!'

'Three thousand *skoed*,' said Little Friar.

'Never.'

'One thousand *skoed*.'

'Done!'

The old woman was buried in Pontrew cemetery, and Little Friar returned to the abbey to tell his story. Large Friar was appalled, his eyes as big as saucers. One thousand *skoed!* He killed his mother instantly, took her to Pontrew, and stood her against a menhir in the market-place. A businessman happened to pass by and noticed a mark on her neck. Someone had bled her.

'Murder! Murder!' cried the businessman. Someone called a policeman and another called a judge. By the end of the day Large Friar was securely locked up in jail.

And then, of course, Little Friar became the Large Friar of Bear Abbey.

ENORI

THE PROBLEM DAUGHTER

Aeons ago there lived a king in the city of Iz who had a very beautiful daughter called Enori. Enori's mother had died and Enori wanted her father to remarry. Her father decided on Fantig.

'I won't marry you until the day you kill Enori,' trumpeted Fantig. In her heart of hearts Fantig was afraid the kingdom would slip through her fingers on Enori's marriage to the first handsome prince who happened along.

The king pondered long and hard. For better or worse, he entrusted Enori to the care of nuns, far away in a remote corner of the land. He killed a dog, and delivered its heart on a plate to Fantig, assuring her it was Enori's heart. They were married without ado.

Next to Brittany, in the country of France, there lived a king who had four sons. Each son left home for a year, in search of adventure. When next they met, each asked the other what adventures they had undertaken, and what lessons they had learned.

'I've learned to shoot with my finger,' said the eldest son, 'and now I can shoot anything at all – ant or giant.'

'I own a fiddle which makes everyone dance,' said the second son. 'I can even raise the dead by playing my fiddle.'

'I'm an expert at climbing heights and plumbing depths,' said the third son.

'I can carry any weight on my shoulders with no trouble at all,' said the little brother.

'Perfect!' said the eldest brother. 'Why don't we go on an adventure, all of us together? The Fearless Four!'

And so it happened that they came to a lofty castle. One brother climbed the ramparts and saw a beautiful princess imprisoned by a noxious serpent. Another brother shot the serpent dead with his finger. The princess was so terrified, she fell to the floor, lifeless. Yet another brother came to her side and played a merry tune on his fiddle, restoring her to life and willing her to dance. Each of the four wanted to marry the princess.

'Take me home to the palace of the King of Napoli,' said the princess. 'He will decide which of you I marry.'

'Let me carry you home,' implored the little brother, 'you and all your treasures.'

The King of Napoli decided on the musician for a son-in-law, since it was he who had revived the princess. They were married, and the other three brothers continued with their adventure.

The King of France had no inkling of their campaigns and was growing impatient with his four sons, wandering the world like four lost souls. Indeed the King of France was so piqued, he gave up on them and put his sons in the hands of Kolevran the Giant. In no time at all Kolevran had caught up with three of the sons and consigned them to the dungeons of his castle. He threw a withered branch onto the courtyard and

bellowed, 'When this branch sprouts fresh young leaves, you're free men! Ha! Ha! Ha!'

Do you still remember Enori? As luck would have it Fantig found her one day in the convent with the nuns, and invited her to the palace of Iz. Fantig hated her to distraction, just for being alive. She would kill Enori even if it were the last thing she achieved on earth. Fantig took Enori for a walk past the castle of Kolevran the Giant, taking Yannig, the servant, as company. When they were walking past a very deep pit right next to the castle, Fantig entreated both to come to her side. 'How charming! Do come and see!'

When Enori was within a hair's breadth of her, Fantig pushed Enori into the pit – straight into the arms of the sons of the King of France! Yannig was so frightened, he soon succumbed to Fantig's bullying, and her strict orders that he should keep his silence.

Each day Yannig carried meat and white bread to the prisoners. When the Queen caught him in the act one morning, she beat him to within an inch of his life. How could she kill Enori? A sorceress might be the answer!

'Take this shirt to Enori,' said the sorceress. 'It will freeze her solid and she can never be revived again.'

Away went Fantig to the castle of Kolevran the Giant, taking with her a rich red shirt for Enori. Enori was transformed into a statue of ice. She fell against the dungeon wall. There she stood as still as stone until the brothers decided to put her in a chest and to sail it far across the seas. Perhaps she would be found by a winsome young prince, and buried in a very beautiful garden.

As the son of the King of Spain walked the seashore one fine spring morning, he was amazed to see a chest washed up onto the beach. He opened the chest and in it lay the most beautiful girl he had ever set eyes on. He wept. It was as much as he could do to bury this lovely girl there and then on the shimmering beach.

He wrapped her in a clean, dry shirt. As he did so she moved, just a fraction. The prince kissed the beautiful girl, and she opened her eyes. He doted on her. The prince insisted that he marry her there and then, out on the seashore.

Enori's father was invited, as was Fantig. However, the wicked Fantig had brought with her to the wedding a pill-box full of magic ointment, ointment which would change Enori into a little blue bird that had the power to compel all the trees around to sprout new leaves. She poured the ointment on Enori's wedding dress, and away flew Enori to the castle of Kolevran the Giant.

The little blue bird stood on the withered branch out in the courtyard, and in the twinkling of an eye the withered branch thrived with freshness and vigour, sprouting fresh green leaves. One of the three brothers touched the little blue bird. It changed into the loveliest young girl imaginable – Enori! They were so happy, they laughed and laughed until they cried.

And then, of course, all four returned to the marriage feast and lived happily ever after!

SCOTLAND

The BLUE FALCON

In the olden times there lived a young huntsman called Mac Iain Direach out in the Western Isles and he was the king's son. There was nothing Mac Iain Direach enjoyed more than stalking deer and often he would shoot a sackful to bring home to his father. But one day Mac Iain Direach's luck changed. It was late afternoon and his sack was empty. He peered far into the distance and saw a blue falcon. He took aim and shot the falcon in its wing, but only a single blue feather fell to the ground. He tucked the blue feather into his belt and took it home to his stepmother as a birthday gift.

Now his stepmother knew very well that the Blue Falcon was a magic bird. She ordered Mac Iain Direach to hunt it with a keen eye until it was caught. 'And don't set foot inside this palace until the Blue Falcon is safely in your bag.'

The following day, although he had zipped up the slopes and stared in this direction and that, Mac Iain Direach hadn't spotted the Blue Falcon. As night fell and the sun tinged the mountain summits red, he sat in the warm heather trying to work out what to do next. Night had closed in when that cunning old fox, Gillie Mairtean, happened to be passing by.

'You're out late,' said Gillie Mairtean. On impulse, Mac Iain Direach told him the whole story. 'Don't worry,' said the fox, 'I know where the falcon lives. The Blue Falcon is owned by the Giant with Five Heads, Five Necks and Five Humps. Why don't you go and work for him, and when the time is ripe, steal the bird! Make sure that no part of it touches the house as you leave. If that happens, you'll be in big trouble. But for the time being, share this supper with me.'

Next morning the two journeyed to the home of the Giant with Five Heads, Five Necks and Five Humps, and Mac Iain Direach offered his services as the huntsman's servant. 'I can manage hounds and hawks better than anyone,' he said.

'Splendid!' bellowed the giant. 'Come inside!'

Everything worked out well. One morning the giant said he wanted to visit his brother who lived over the mountain. What an opportunity! Once the giant was well out of sight Mac Iain Direach snatched the falcon and opened the back door in flight. The Blue Falcon spread its wings as it saw the bright sunshine, and the tip of one wing touched the doorpost. The doorpost screeched so shrilly the giant heard it clearly on the far side of the mountain. This would be the end of Mac Iain Direach. In two shakes of a cat's tail the Giant with Five Heads, Five Necks and Five Humps was back on his own doorstep.

'Thief! You were just about to steal my falcon!'

'I was,' admitted Mac Iain Direach. 'I'm very sorry, but you see I can't return home without taking the Blue Falcon to my stepmother.'

Mac Iain Direach expected the giant to hammer him so hard with his fist that his feet would sink into the ground. But no.

'I'll give you the falcon in return for the White Sword of Light owned by the Big Women of Jura,' said the giant.

Mac Iain Direach walked all day in search of the Big Women but didn't find them. He sat in the warm heather as the sun set.

'You're out late this evening again,' – it was Gillie Mairtean, the fox. Mac Iain Direach told him his story.

'Don't worry,' consoled the fox, 'I know where they live.'

The next morning the fox turned himself into a boat and off they went to the home of the Big Women. Mac Iain Direach offered himself as a cleaner and so it was that he polished their furniture and scrubbed their floors until they shone. And yes, eventually he was allowed to rub the White Sword of Light. What an opportunity! He rested the sword on his shoulder and opened the back door. But the tip of the blade touched the door lintel, and it screeched brazenly throughout the land.

'Thief! You were just about to steal our sword!'

'I was,' admitted Mac Iain Direach. 'I'm very sorry, but you see I can't return home without first taking this sword to the giant, who will give me the falcon to present to my stepmother.'

Mac Iain Direach expected the Big Women to drive the sword through his heart. But no.

'We'll give you the sword in return for the Yellow Filly which belongs to the King of Ireland,' said the Big Women.

Mac Iain Direach walked all day but wasn't even half way to Ireland by nightfall. Exhausted, he sat in the warm heather. Who should pass by but Gillie Mairtean, full of wisdom as always. Early next morning Gillie Mairtean turned himself into a boat and was moored in Ireland before lunch.

Mac Iain Direach found work in the stables of the King of Ireland with the amazing Yellow Filly. One morning the king went off hunting. What an opportunity! Mac Iain Direach saddled the filly and opened the stable door. As soon as she saw open country the Yellow Filly neighed excitedly and swished her tail, only just catching the doorpost with its tip. The doorpost screeched at the top of its voice and the king returned from the hunt instantly.

'Thief! You were just about to steal my filly!'

'I was,' admitted Mac Iain Direach. 'I'm very sorry, but you see I can't return home without first taking the Yellow Filly to the Big Women, who will give me the sword to take to the giant, who will give me the Blue Falcon to present to my stepmother.'

Mac Iain Direach expected the king to hang him. But no.

'I'll give you the Yellow Filly if I can marry the King of France's daughter,' said the King of Ireland.

Mac Iain Direach walked until nightfall but hadn't covered a quarter of the ground to the French border. He sat in the warm heather to nurse his toes. At last Gillie Mairtean appeared and promised to help him over to France.

With his feet firmly on French soil Gillie Mairtean sent his friend to the king's palace with the message that Mac Iain Direach's ship had been wrecked on the beach. The king, his wife and daughter came down to the seashore to inspect the damage. Gillie Mairtean was there too, in the form of a vessel which had seen better days.

'But what lovely melodies!' gasped the princess. 'May I step on deck to meet the musicians?'

As she and Mac Iain Direach stepped on board the ship, it slipped quietly out to sea and before long they were out of sight.

'I'm very sorry,' said Mac Iain Direach, 'but I'm taking you to Ireland to be the king's wife.'

'I'd rather be your wife,' said the princess. Mac Iain Direach had rather hoped she would say that, and smiled.

Once in Ireland, Gillie Mairtean requested the princess to wait on the beach until he and Mac Iain Direach returned. Gillie Mairtean took the form of a beautiful woman and walked with his friend to the king's palace. The King of Ireland was much taken with the winsome young redhead, and thanked Mac Iain Direach from the bottom of his heart for bringing her to him. He placed the Yellow Filly's reins in Mac Iain Direach's hand, and the

young huntsman led the filly down to the beach. In a flash Gillie Mairtean turned himself back into a fox, bit the king's hand, fled down to the beach, turned himself into a ship, and sailed with Mac Iain Direach, the daughter of the King of France, and the Yellow Filly on board, far away across the ocean to the Big Women of Jura's home.

There, Gillie Mairtean turned himself into a filly and the Big Women were very proud to own such an impressive pony. Mac Iain Direach accepted the White Sword of Light from their hands with no fuss at all. Each of the Big Women mounted their new pony and set off for a ride. Gillie Mairtean tossed all seven over a cliff.

The three travelled onwards to visit the Giant with Five Heads, Five Necks and Five Humps. Gillie Mairtean transformed himself into a sharp sword. The giant swapped the Blue Falcon for the sword but the sword turned on the giant and killed him.

Mac Iain Direach had a fiancée, a filly, a sword, and a falcon. As he approached home he held the sword between his eyes for fear his stepmother planned on tricking him – and that is exactly what kept Mac Iain Direach safe from her spells. His stepmother was transformed into a bundle of firewood and that was that.

Of course, Mac Iain Direach married the daughter of the King of France, and yes, they lived happily ever after.

TAM LIN

One mellow autumn day, the valley ablaze with yellowing beech leaves, a young girl slipped away from her father's castle and ran all the way to Caterhaugh. She was visiting a well of icy cold water owned by the fairy folk.

As the girl kneeled at the well, a shadow fell over her. There was a large, white stallion sporting a golden saddle where no horse or saddle had stood the previous instant. The girl was alarmed and her heart beat faster, but she admitted to nothing of the sort. Instead, she plucked a rose from a nearby bush. As she turned on her heels intent on running back to her father a young man appeared before her wearing clothes of green and gold, where no man or robes had been the previous instant.

'Janet, that rose is mine,' said the young man.

'You know my name!' said Janet. 'And what is your name?'

'Tam Lin.'

When Tam Lin smiled at her, Janet's chilly heart melted. On such a cheerful day, with the sun high in the heavens, she forgot all her fears. The two lingered at the well until nightfall, chatting and holding hands, as young

lovers do. At last, Janet walked slowly home, dreaming beautiful dreams, her eyes as bright as the stars in the sky and her heart had a warm beat to it.

She walked into her father's palace, but the Earl, her father, was uneasy.

'It's high time you married a fine young man instead of wasting your days gallivanting about the countryside.'

'There isn't one of your knights I'd want to marry,' said Janet. 'I love Tam Lin.'

The Earl couldn't believe his own ears. 'One of the fairy folk! You don't know what you're saying!'

'I know very well that I love Tam Lin who owns the most beautiful horse and the most beautiful saddle in the world,' said Janet. Before her father could say anything further Janet ran out of the palace, all the way to Caterhaugh. She plucked a rose and Tam Lin appeared before her once more.

'Are you one of the fairy folk, Tam Lin? Tell me the honest truth.'

'My grandfather is Earl Roxburgh,' said Tam Lin. 'As I was returning home one day from hunting I fell off my horse into a fairy ring. The Fairy Queen took me to her castle to become one of her knights.'

'Could you ever return to Caterhaugh to live?'

'Only you could release me from this enchanted kingdom, Janet. Tonight is Hallowe'en when the fairy folk march and ride in procession. Be here at the spring at midnight and when you see the Queen at the head of the procession and all her knights following, allow the black horse to pass by, so too the bay horse. But run to the white stallion that follows. I am that rider. Hold me tightly, and never let go!'

'I will do everything as you say, Tam Lin.'

'Take great care. The fairy folk will not give way easily. They're certain to transform me into a thousand and one different objects in your hand, but whatever happens, don't let go. When I'm eventually transformed into a red-hot cinder throw me into the well and I'll be a man once again, at long last. Wrap me in a cloak and all will be well.'

Janet returned to the castle and stayed there until just before midnight. She wrapped her cloak about her and set off for the well. The path was as familiar to her as the back of her hand, and in spite of the sooty-black night she stepped brightly past the black cow, the black heather, and the black gorse, every step of the way to the well. The water was as cold as death. Janet had never in her life been as frightened as she was then. Fighting the fairies! Whatever had come over her?

She could see them coming, the horses' manes a parade of tiny golden bells ringing and chiming. The Queen rode past. The black horse went past, as did the bay horse. The white stallion! Janet jumped out to him, and pulled the fairy knight into her arms. Instantly the knight became an agile little lizard, flitting and darting through her fingers. Janet took firm hold of its head, and tightened her grasp. The lizard changed into a long, writhing serpent intent on killing her but Janet hugged it close, as if she were embracing Tam Lin himself. The serpent was transformed into a grizzly bear with sharp paws which tore at Janet's flesh. She clung to the shaggy coat until the bear turned into a rapacious lion with sharp claws. Janet held fast to its mane and held her ground. But that too was short-lived. The lion became a white-hot bar of iron in the palm of her hand and she almost threw it into the water. But she held fast. When she was almost beside herself with pain the iron bar changed into a live coal, which Janet threw into the icy well with all her might.

The fairy folk were incensed. They hurtled around her in agitation, wincing and flinching about her head, groaning and screeching inarticulately. Tam Lin climbed out of the well as naked as the day he was born. Janet threw her cloak over him and Tam Lin fell into her arms. The fairy folk settled into an uneasy silence. Only the Queen could find the strength to speak.

'You have won Tam Lin. You have won the world's best knight.' At that, the Queen uttered a single venomous screech before disappearing into the darkness bearing away all her followers.

Tam Lin and Janet lingered long in the shadow of the well and the rose bushes, kissing and holding hands as not-so-new lovers do.

THE ISLE OF MAN

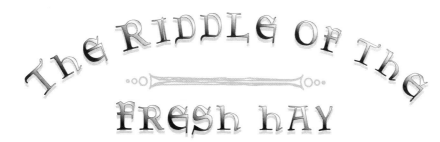

THE RIDDLE OF THE FRESH HAY

A long time ago the ruler of the Isle of Man was also a magician. His name was Manannán. Manannán lived in a castle high on the slopes of Barule. From his bedroom window he could see far out to sea in all directions. He could scan the beach where he moored his magic coracle, the Wave-Sweeper, and he could keep a sharp eye on his horse. (His horse could pull Manannán's chariot over the ocean even when the waves were at their most dangerous.) And that was not all. Amongst Manannán's other possessions were a cloak and helmet of invisibility. When he wore his cloak and helmet no one could see even the tip of his toe. The king was also a notorious shape-shifter. If he wished to rush from one end of the island to the other, Manannán would take upon himself the shape of the Manx coat of arms, three legs forming a sort of wheel, and roll swiftly across the island.

Once a year his people had to pay Manannán a rent of fresh hay. Each head of household had to walk to the top of Barule to pay one bundle of the best hay on his farmland. The rent was only a single sheaf because

Manx farms were small and the farmers very poor.

One summer the harvest had been particularly bad. The sun had hardly shone out from behind the clouds, and what with the mists arching around the coastland and the rain lashing the fells of Barule, it made for a rotten hay harvest altogether. Each farmer to the last man produced inferior quality hay. Yet, they had to deliver their best sheaf to the door of Manannán's castle.

Amongst the Manx farmers was Finn Cregeen. Finn was a gossipy little so-and-so who enjoyed his own grumpy ways. More than anything in the world, he loved sulking and scheming, criticising and complaining until his tongue was parched – and still he had plenty to moan about.

Finn Cregeen hated hard work. He hated mowing his meadows; he hated spreading out the grass to dry; he hated reaping the harvest. But he, like everyone else, had to deposit his best sheaf of hay in Manannán's haystack.

'Manannán will get no more from me than the tiniest, puniest sheaf of hay I can find on my farm. Why should I work my fingers to the bone and carry my best sheaf to the top of Barule in order to feed Manannán's cattle?'

He set off on his journey muttering under his breath. By the time he was half way up the steep path to the castle his mind was a cauldron of black thoughts. On reaching Manannán's barn, he threw down the hay at his feet.

Finn Cregeen's heart was full of resentment.

'Why should I be anyone's servant?' Finn Cregeen questioned himself. 'All this good hay up here in the castle, and I with next to nothing back home.'

Finn took a chance. As soon as Manannán had turned his back on Finn Cregeen to speak to members of his retinue, Finn snatched two bundles of fine strong hay. He ran as fast as his legs would carry him down the mountainside and through his own back door.

'No one saw me! Not a soul!' said Finn, and he almost smiled.

But that was where Finn Cregeen was wrong. Not one of the king's retinue had seen him, that was true enough. But at the very last instant Manannán turned his head and saw Finn snatching up the best bundles of hay on the Isle of Man before scrambling down Barule with the wind humming in his ears.

The next morning Finn Cregeen went to feed his cattle. He threw the best feed in the land into the stall but it was no use. The cattle would have none of it. Finn returned to the cowshed at mid-day: the hay was still untouched. By nightfall the cattle were lowing fretfully, half starved. There was nothing for it but empty the stall and re-fill it with hay from Finn's own barn.

'Tomorrow I'll mix my own hay with the stolen hay,' said Finn Cregeen. 'That's what I'll do.'

But when Finn approached the cowsheds the following morning the stench of rotten hay came out from under the door to meet him. Not a blade of grass was fit fodder for his cattle. It would all have to be burned. Finn recognized the hand of Manannán the magician. He had seen, after all.

Finn Cregeen would have to walk the steep path to the castle of Manannán to apologize. Manannán listened in silence to Finn Cregeen. 'What a wretched man you are. Too lazy to grow good quality hay, yet agile enough to run down the paths of Barule clutching two bundles of best Manx hay. I forgive you this time, Finn Cregeen, but let this be a warning to you and to all the people of the Isle of Man: DON'T EVER STEAL OR CHEAT!'

Winter came hard that year to Finn Cregeen's farmstead, but by the spring Finn Cregeen had turned over a new leaf. He worked diligently all summer long. When the time came to deliver Manannán's rent, there wasn't a better sheaf of hay in all the island than that of Finn Cregeen.

The Five Fishermen

One summer's day Finlo Cooil and his four genial brothers went out fishing. They were hoping for a good catch of fish and a hearty supper. So they busied themselves with the fish-hooks and fishnets, and sailed out to sea. They baited hooks, pulled in fish, fed the screaming gulls with scraps, and in no time at all they were ready to head for home.

Quite unexpectedly Finlo heard a strange sound. Someone nearby was singing. It was a soulful melody, heady and intoxicating. Finlo had never before heard such a song, not of man or bird. His heart ached.

'That is the most beautiful song I've ever heard,' said Finlo.

'Pardon?' Finlo's brothers could hear nothing at all over the screech of the gulls and the dub-dubbing of the waves against the fishing boat.

'O-o-h-h-!' groaned the eldest son. 'A mermaid! Whistle, everyone, before she throws a spell on Finlo and lures him out to sea.'

The four brothers whistled and sang, sang and whistled frantically, but Finlo Cooil just sat there, starry-eyed and still. The brothers shouted themselves hoarse, rowing away from the black rocks, away from the thrill of the sad song. As they came in view of the harbour the brothers fell silent and Finlo was soon back on dry land.

The following morning the brothers went fishing. Finlo stared at the black rocks in the distance until his eyes were sore but could hear nothing of that sad song. Finlo listened for the melody until his ears ached, but no notes came over the water. And so it was for days, for weeks - his brothers catching all the fish and chatting merrily away to protect Finlo from the charm of the mermaid's song.

In time, Finlo forgot all about the mermaid with the golden voice, and his brothers allowed him out fishing on his own. Quite by accident Finlo found himself fishing one day within a stone's throw of the black rocks. He heard the sweet song. Something of his brothers' remonstrations came to mind and he began rowing towards the shore. But the song filled his thoughts and soon the rowing stopped. Finlo was spellbound.

There on the smooth black rock was the most beautiful woman in the whole wide world. Her hair was the colour of gorse and she had two pink cheeks the colour of foxgloves. Finlo's heart puffed up with the love

of a mermaid.

'Would you care for a ride in my fishing boat?' asked Finlo.

'There's a beautiful island out at sea. I would love to visit it, more than anything in the world,' said the mermaid.

'Is there? I never saw it,' ventured Finlo, but the mermaid sang her enchanted song before Finlo could finish his sentence. Without another word, Finlo rowed out to sea.

The mermaid sang night and day, Finlo rowing further out to sea by the hour. He was charmed by the bewitching smile of the loveliest woman in the world and her hauntingly tender song.

After a long journey they moored the fishing boat in the harbour of the distant island. Finlo Cooil carried his new friend to a shining castle at the far end of the kingdom. Inside the castle was a brilliantly lit room, full of golden-haired young women with garlands of flowers in their curls. They wore azure cloaks of rustling silk, and torques of shells and coral about their necks. Each one sang and smiled.

In a far corner of the room sat a group of hunched-up old men, their clothes torn and their beards in knots. Each had a wheezy chest which rattled like rusty cans.

'Put me down on that large shell, Finlo,' said the mermaid. 'There's plenty of room for both of us there. And take some of this magic drink after such a long journey.' She smiled her smile.

'Don't drink a single drop, Finlo, my child,' said a rusty voice in his ear, 'or you'll spend the rest of your days wandering about this castle as I do. I have a wife and children on the Isle of Man. I shall never see them again. Not a single drop, my son!'

The mermaid was very angry with the ragged old man. When Finlo detected her anger the spell was broken. Finlo remembered the words of his four genial brothers and threw the magic drink as far away from him as possible. He jumped down from the shell and ran all the way to the harbour calling out his brothers' names over and over again. But the harbour was empty! His fishing boat had disappeared! He plunged himself into the cold waves and swam for his life out into the open sea. He swam and was blown by the wind for days and weeks until one day he reached the Isle of Man.

When he eventually dragged himself up from the beach he looked like an old, old man. With the sun warm on his back and the seagulls screeching above his head he saw his own reflection in the sea of glass and was frightened out of his wits. But until this very day the stars still twinkle in the eyes of Finlo Cooil, and if ever you visit the Isle of Man you may catch a glimpse of him sitting on the beach staring out to sea, listening for the mermaid's song. But if ever you catch its strains, don't be tempted to follow in their wake.

CORNWALL

The Giants of Treen

In the olden days there lived in Treen a family of friendly giants. Although they were kindly folk they were also distinctly odd, as giants tend to be. Their work was to protect the neighbourhood against enemy attacks. They were also responsible for raising a new generation of giants to take their place. Then the young giants would protect the people of Treen when the old giants were dead. In times of peace the Giants of Treen had nothing to do.

There were two Treen giants in this period - Mr Giant and Mrs Giant. Since Mrs Giant didn't have enough to keep her occupied for long she plagued Mr Giant all day, and because Mr Giant hadn't much to do, he grew fat and lazy.

'You lazy good-for-nothing! Go and shake the rocks for an hour or two before lunch. That should stretch your sinews and get the blood running faster through your veins!'

Mr Giant would trudge down to the lofty rocks and shake them easily enough with the tip of his finger. The largest rock was only thirty feet, and Mr Giant was at least forty feet without his boots.

After lunch Mrs Giant might say, 'Blockhead! Swim a mile or two out to sea to fish for congers. I need their fat to bake a few cakes for tea.'

Obediently Mr Giant would swim out to sea and in an hour or two he would bring her home a string of black, slippery eels. Then he would sit in his favourite chair down on the beach to wait for his tea. Sometimes he would doze off in the warm sun, until Mrs Giant pelted him with stones to wake him up.

'You sluggish oaf!' she would bellow, hurling sharp stones at Mr Giant. He would wake up with an almighty headache, and with little desire to munch conger-cake for tea.

'What a quarrelsome woman!' sighed Mr Giant. But on the quiet he sympathised with her. All she wanted was a baby, and she didn't have one.

'Why don't you snatch one of the Maen Giant's babies?' asked one of the wise men of Treen. 'He has so many children one small baby would never be missed. Or what about the toddlers? One of those would do splendidly!'

'Perfect!' said Mrs Giant. 'Before long I will have the world's best baby to bring up. That lout of a husband of mine can tickle his belly and wipe his nose, and I can sit outdoors dandling the child in the afternoon sun. The house will be higgledy-piggledy and I will have lots and lots to do. Perfect!'

The old witch of Treen was chosen to steal the baby. Off she went after tea in the direction of Maen. A little before sundown she noticed two or three human children and one giant's son coming down the road. The giant's child was about four years old. Just right.

'Would you like to see these pretty buttons?' asked the witch. The children were playing bob and the witch's buttons would be ideal for the game. The giant's son had his hands full of shiny buttons.

'I'm on my way to Cowloe to search for limpets and winkles,' said the witch. 'Would you like to come with me?'

'Thank you, old woman,' said the people-children, 'but we have to go home before dark or we'll be smacked and sent to bed without supper.'

'I won't be smacked, old woman. I'll come with you,' said the giant's child.

'Then away we go!' said the witch taking the child's hand and leading him slowly along the path. When the child tired, the witch changed into a horse and trotted with the child on her back for a mile or two to give him a bit of a rest. On they went, hand in hand, every step of the path to Treen.

When the child reached his new home his new mother was as happy as a lark. Whenever the child cried, Mrs Giant rushed over to the bed hewn into the rock and sang her song in a voice you could hear in Scotland. All summer Mr Giant took the child sea-fishing. Sometimes Mr Giant took him swimming. At other times they would watch the cormorants, or feed the gulls.

Summer became winter and winter summer, and before long the child had grown tall, as tall as Mr Giant. Every year Mrs Giant loved Little Giant a little bit more, and every year Little Giant's heart beat somewhat mor rapidly each time he saw his mother. Mrs Giant and Little Giant had become very close friends. Mr Giant was left out of their card games and it became as plain as day that Mrs Giant was bored to death by him. Mrs Giant was becoming a surly and crotchety wife once more, complaining so much that it cut him to the heart.

One day in the depths of winter, the winds sharp on the Cornish coast, Mr Giant set off to buy provisions. 'Meet me in an hour's time,' said Mr Giant. 'I'll need a hand to carry the load home.'

Mr Giant bought five cows, six sacks of flour, seven gallons of milk, eight flagons of honey, nine measures of butter, and ten bags of potatoes for supper. On his journey into town Mr Giant saw the schoolmaster, he chatted to the doctor, he waved to the farmers in the market, but he could find not a hair of his wife or foster-son. He carried his load on his back until he groaned with the pain in his ribs. Where were Mrs Giant and Little Giant?

Those two unfriendly giants had forgotten all about Mr Giant and his supper. But they soon remembered when they heard him coming, a quarter of a mile off, ranting and raving in pain. Mrs Giant had done it this time. Mr Giant would not let her get away with this.

Mrs Giant prepared herself for a fight. She stood in wait for her husband, grinning a tiresome grin. As Mr Giant rounded the corner Mrs Giant punched him on the nose and Mr Giant and his supper fell headlong over the cliff. Mrs Giant threw her apron over her head to avoid hearing Mr Giant's groans. His skull was smashed to smithereens.

But before Mr Giant died he asked the powers to turn his wife into stone. And so it happened that Mrs Giant became a cold black stone that could never move again.

The Ghost of Stithians

Way back in the time when ghost stories were true, a sprightly woman called Jenny Hendy lived all by herself in a thatched cottage in the parish of Stithians in Cornwall. It was a comfortable house with a garden and small orchard, and enough land to keep a pig and a few sheep, a cow and a few hens. She had no husband or children, but unfortunately she had a cousin or two here and there who were more than willing to tell her how to spend her savings.

'You won't live for ever,' they assured her.

'Don't you worry about that,' said the sprightly old woman. 'I'm in no hurry to change my little world.' Then all her relations to the ninth generation would turn their eyes to the heavens and shake their heads in disappointment.

Before long, Jenny Hendy became firm friends with a young man who worked on the farm next door. His name was Robin and every day after finishing work on the farm he would pop over to Jenny's to give her a hand. At the end of every week Robin handed his money to Jenny's care. She told him she would add to his savings, from her own pocket, when Robin brought home a tidy little woman for his wife.

Late one Saturday afternoon Robin called on Jenny Hendy and found her sitting dead at the kitchen table. Goodness gracious! Robin and one of the neighbours searched high and low but not a trace of Jenny Hendy's wealth or of Robin's savings could they find. There wasn't a penny to be found in all the house, not in the rafters, not in the cellars, and certainly not enough to pay the undertakers. Robin footed the bills from his own pocket and no one caught even a glimpse of the little old woman's cousins on that sad day.

However, all and sundry knew that Jenny Hendy had bequeathed her home to Robin and so Robin moved into the comfortable little house with a garden and a small orchard, to fatten the pigs and tend the stock. The villagers soon advised him on a way of finding the missing money too - summon the help of the witch of Helston.

'Two pounds,' said Tammy the witch. Having settled on terms, and having waited until after dark, Robin made his way to the parish church to

meet her. Although it was a very dark night Robin's face was as white as snow. Tammy babbled away incessantly but when Robin asked her what she was saying she snapped, 'Be quiet, will you? I'm speaking to the spirits and hate being interrupted.' She turned to him abruptly and grabbed his arm. 'You're not afraid, are you?'

By the time they got to the lychgate Robin was full of misgivings. 'Take three swigs of this before we start work,' urged Tammy knocking back the brandy, her head in a whirl.

On they went, through the gate and up the path to the church door. 'Don't be afraid, not even of the Devil himself. Tie this hanky over your eyes and you'll see nothing of him or of his wicked servants. Their eyes are like saucers of fire and their horns sharp enough to cut bread. But you're not afraid, are you?'

'I'm not afraid of fire or of bread,' said Robin, his knees knocking.

'This graveyard is full of spirits, as you well know. Look! There's a row of them sitting astride the roof-ridge! But it's time we visited Jenny Hendy's grave and raised her ghost.'

Something groaned behind a tombstone. Robin felt his blood run cold and his hair stand on end. 'I can't bear any more! Keep the money! I'm going home!' Robin thrust the two pounds into the witch's bony hands

and was out through the lychgate in a flash.

After that fiasco Robin was very nervous of being alone in his comfortable little house. When he left for the fields in the early morning he would rather go without his lunch than return to the house at twelve to prepare it. One day, coming home at the end of a long working day he thought he could see Jenny Hendy standing in the doorway, wearing a jaunty sailor's cap. Robin was only a shadow of his former self and was so terrified he could hardly breathe.

'How are you, Robin?' asked the figure in the doorway. 'I thought I'd look you up since my ship is docked at Falmouth. May I stay here tonight?'

'Goodness me! Cousin Jack! It's you! Back from sea!' Robin had never been so relieved, or so pleased to see him. Before long he had told Jack his tale, in the light of a cheery log fire.

'Hmm, Tammy the witch! I think I'll pay her a call sometime tomorrow. She may raise the ghost of Jenny Hendy yet,' pondered Jack.

After supper the following evening Robin and Jack went to visit Tammy the witch of Helston. It was settled that she would carry out the work for two pounds, and so they made their way to the church soon after sundown.

'Is it the Devil
and his friend making that
clatter?' asked Jack.

'Certainly,' assured
Tammy, 'but don't be afraid,
I'll look after you.'

Suddenly the
clamouring stopped and
all was quiet. Tammy drew
a circle around Jack, telling
him to keep within it for

fear of being snatched by the ghosts. Tammy raised her magic cudgel and chanted an incantation long enough to frighten the cats away. She invoked the spirit of Jenny Hendy.

Groans came from behind the gravestone and a white shape loomed up. It moved slowly towards them, complaining fretfully. The hair on Jack's head stood on end, and trembled in the night air. The white shape came nearer still, demanding to know why it had been disturbed on such a frosty evening. 'I'll plague you every night of your life for this,' said the spirit in a hoary voice, reaching out its bony fingers to the sailor's throat.

Jack punched it on the nose, and drew blood! Jack wasn't a bit afraid of a spirit who stank of whisky and tobacco! It was Jemmy, Tammy's drunken husband!

'You swindlers! If you don't give Robin his money back this instant, I'll break every bone in your body!' thundered Jack.

'No!' pleaded Tammy. 'It was only a bit of leg-pulling - Jemmy clapping saucepan lids and dressing up as a ghost. No harm was done and we'll repay every penny before dawn tomorrow.'

You should never cheat on your neighbours, but some good did come of it all. The story spread far and wide that Tammy the witch of Helston had raised the spirit of Jenny Hendy and that she would soon name the culprits who had stolen her money. Worse still, if the total sum wasn't returned within the month she would blind the thieves in their left eye. In no time at all Robin found bundles of money thrown into the cowshed, and one or two in the hen-runs too, but not one of the sprightly little woman's cousins was spotted anywhere near the house ever again after that.

One night a storm blew up and the thatched roof was blown off part of Robin's house. There, wedged into the wall on the gable-end of the house, was the sprightly old woman's will. She had left all her possessions to Robin. Before long another sprightly little woman came to live in the comfortable house with a garden and orchard, and the two lived happily, long after Jack kissed them both goodbye and sailed out of Falmouth, far away to sea.